Note from the Founder & Co-Founders

Bharat Babies was founded in late 2014 with a simple mission in mind - to produce developmentally appropriate children's books that tell the story of India's heritage. *Hanuman and the Orange Sun* is our flagship book, which tells the story of a Telugu-American girl, Harini, who is learning about Hanuman for the first time. We hope you love this story as much as we do!

For the love of reading,
Sailaja, Megan, & SriVani

Author Note

Hanuman and the Orange Sun is the re-telling of a story based on ancient Hindu lore where Hanuman mistakes the sun for a giant mango.

For Michael and Emmett, for their charm and wit.
- Tim Palin

To my beloved godparents, Pat and Ted Levine.
- Amy Maranville

For Ojo.
- Sailaja Joshi

HANUMAN AND THE ORANGE SUN

WORDS BY
AMY MARANVILLE

PICTURES BY
TIM PALIN

www.mascotbooks.com | www.bharatbabies.com

Hanuman and the Orange Sun

For more information, please contact:
Mascot Books | 560 Herndon Parkway #120 | Herndon, VA 20170
info@mascotbooks.com

Library of Congress Control Number: 2015907452

CPSIA Code: PRT0615A
ISBN-13: 978-1-63177-199-6

Printed in the United States

This is Harini. Harini loves chipmunks, sailboats, and playing in the summer sun. Every morning when it is warm, Harini wakes up, brushes her teeth, and runs outside to play.

One day, after a bright and sunny morning outside, Harini felt particularly hungry. She ran into her mother's office.

"Amma, Amma, can I have a *paratha* for lunch?"

"Of course, my *kanna*, my sweetheart."

"And a cheese stick?"

"Of course, *kanna.*"

"And an orange?"

"My, you are as hungry as Hanuman Dada today."

"Who?" asked Harini as she pulled on her mother's arm.

"Hanuman Dada. Come, I will tell you the story while we eat."

Harini and her mother went into the kitchen. There, Harini climbed into her tower to help her mother make lunch. While they rolled the *paratha*, Harini's mother began the story of Hanuman Dada and the orange sun.

"Before he grew to be a tall, strong god," she said, "Hanuman Dada was just a baby in his crib. One morning, Hanuman Dada woke up and was very hungry…"

He looked up and saw a bright, bright orange way up high in the sky. *Ah*, he thought to himself, *a big, juicy orange. I will fly up and take a bite.*

So Hanuman Dada stretched his legs – one, two – and squatted down. He swished his tail back and forth, and took aim. Then he pushed off with his legs and jumped up into the sky.

Hanuman Dada flew into the air. Up, up, up, he went, past the trunks of trees,

past the tree tops,

past the birds,

over the clouds,

and up, up, up

until he reached the sun.

He felt the heat of the sun on his face. *Hmm*, he thought, *what a lovely, warm, juicy orange this will be. I think I will eat the whole thing in just one bite.*

So Hanuman Dada opened his mouth wide, wide, wide, and…

CHOMP!

He ate the sun up in just one bite.

But with the sun in his mouth, it could not shine down on the Earth.

Everything was dark, dark, dark.

"Ah!" cried Hanuman Dada in alarm.

"I cannot see!"

Hanuman Dada wasn't the only one who couldn't see. "Who turned out the lights?" cried the gods in the sky. Panicked, they called to their leader to bring back the sun. "Indra, King of the gods, help us!"

And Indra cried, "A ferocious monster has eaten our sun! I will strike it down!" So he lifted his *vajra*, his lightning bolt, high above his head and threw it at poor Hanuman Dada.

Boom!

The bolt of lightning struck Hanuman Dada, and he cried out in shock. As he opened his mouth, the sun came out and shone brightly again.

Hanuman Dada tumbled down, down, down through the clouds, past the birds, past the tree tops, past the trunks of trees…and back to Earth where he landed with a big

THUD.

"OUCH!" said Hanuman Dada, and he started to cry.

His father, Vayu the Wind God, heard him crying. He ran to his son and cradled him. "Why have the gods done this to my son?" he shouted, angrily.

But Indra said nothing.

Again Vayu demanded, "Tell me why this has happened!"

Again, no one answered.

Finally, Vayu stomped his foot and said, "If no one answers me, I will stop the winds!" But still, Indra did not answer.

So Vayu stopped the wind. The trees were still, the crops were still, the oceans were still, and the whole Earth was desert hot.

Indra realized his mistake and felt sorry. So he and the other gods came down to Earth, and brought special gifts to Hanuman Dada.

"… And I bet you can guess which one was his favorite," Harini's Amma said.

Harini smiled and bit into her own juicy orange. "Did the Wind God bring back the winds?"

"He did. And Hanuman learned a valuable lesson. Do you know what that lesson was, *kanna*?"

"Be careful what you bite?" guessed Harini.

Harini's mother laughed and gave her a hug. "That, but also to think before you act because you are more powerful than you know."

"Do you mean I have super powers?" Harini asked, "I could throw vajra or bite the sun?"

"Maybe not yet, my love. But if you put your mind to it, I bet you could accomplish anything. And when you can, I hope you will be thoughtful and use your strength well."

THE END

About the Author

Amy Maranville has a Bachelor of Arts in English literature and anthropology from Smith College, and a Master's in Children's Literature from Simmons College in Boston. She is a passionate believer in the importance of diversity in the books we give to our children, and is proud to present positive images of diversity in her stories. Amy lives in Somerville, Massachusetts with her husband, young son, and beloved basset hound.

About the Illustrator

After graduating from Salem State College, Tim started his design career in event and marketing/promotions agencies in and around Boston. When he made the move to New York City as Promotional Art Director for *ELLE Girl* magazine, he worked with fashion brands including America's Next Top Model, Ecko Unltd., and TJMaxx. He also designed for *Stuff* and *Vibe* magazines. Eventually, Tim moved into book publishing as Senior Designer for Disney Editions/Disney Press. He's art directed, designed, and produced books for both the children's and adult contemporary markets for publishers including Scholastic Books, Blue Apple Books, Girl Scouts of America, Disney Press, Bill Smith Group/Houghton Mifflin, Race Point Publishing, Sterling Innovation, Hinkler Books, Enchanted Lion Books, PrintMatters, Thunder Bay Press, Cantata Learning, The Book Shop Ltd., and Octane Press. As an illustrator for the children's publishing market, Tim is thrilled to be working with Bharat Babies for this very special endeavor.